For Nicky Potter

FLY

on the wall

Front endpaper

In 484 BC young Ambrosia picks olives with her friends.

Back endpaper

In 463 BC Ambrosia shows her son an owl in that same olive tree.

Researched on location at the British Museum.
Historical consultant: Dr Thorsten Opper, Curator of Greek
and Roman Antiquities at the British Museum.

Find out more about this book at www.mickandbrita.com

No living creatures were harmed during the making of this book.

Fly on the Wall: Greek Hero copyright © Frances Lincoln Limited 2007
Text and Illustrations copyright © Mick Manning and Brita Granström 2007

First published in Great Britain in 2007 and in the USA in 2008 by
Frances Lincoln Children's Books, 4 Torriano Mews,
Torriano Avenue, London NW5 2RZ

www.franceslincoln.com

British Library Cataloguing in Publication Data available on request

ISBN: 978-1-84507-683-2

The illustrations for this book are watercolour and pencil

Printed in Singapore

9 8 7 6 5 4 3 2 1

GREEK HERO

MICK MANNING
BRITA GRANSTRÖM

CONTENTS

Who were the Greeks?	6
Meet the Greeks	7
Victory	8
Homeward Bound	10
Campfire Stories	12
Deliveries	14
Home Life	16
Theatre	18
Temple of the Gods	20
School Days	22
Wedding Day	24
Greek Women	26
Market Place	28
Sparta	30
Olympia	32
The Games	34
End of the Greeks	36
What the Greeks Left Behind	36
Glossary & Index	36

F

FRANCES LINCOLN
CHILDREN'S BOOKS

WHO WERE THE GREEKS?

Ancient Greece began around 1100 BC. Greece, a mountainous mainland with hundreds of small islands dotted around its seas, was divided into 'city states' each having their own ruler. These states included Athens, Sparta and many more. Ancient Greeks loved beauty, music, literature, drama, philosophy, politics and art, as well as battle, glory and sport. This book is set in 479 BC in the period of the Greek wars with Persia, a time of great victories for Greece that began with the famous battle of Marathon. Later with the naval battle of Salamis and the land battle of Plataea, the Greeks defeated the Persians. But Athens at this time had been burned to the ground...

ANCIENT
GREECE

MEET THE GREEKS

Our story begins at the victory at Plataea in 479 BC. Trade between the islands is thriving. Let's look in on some of the Ancient Greeks and see how they live their lives.

Ambrosia
Lykon's daughter

Agathon
A hoplite warrior

Lykon
Ambrosia's father

Hektor
Ambrosia's brother

Zoe
A slave

Pelagon
A Greek Philosopher

Ariston
A teacher

Demetra
Agathon's mother

After the sea battle of Salamis in 480 BC, the Persian king and his navy retreated, leaving his army behind!

All Athenian men had to serve time in the army. But Spartans had to join the army for life.

"Retreat!"
"The battle is lost!"

VICTORY

The Greeks and the Persians have been fighting for years but now, at last, the Greeks have beaten the invaders. This is a huge victory for the Greek states. Now there will be peace. Soldiers like Agathon can go home.

Persian warriors

Agathon fought bravely, now he wants to go home. He is asking the merchant Lykon for a lift.

Greeks fight with spears and short stabbing swords.

There were battles against the Persians at Marathon in 490 BC, and at Salamis. The final battle was fought at Plataea in 479 BC.

We know about historical events like this because they were written down by a Greek called Herodotus.

HOMEWARD BOUND

Lykon's children, Ambrosia and Hektor, are aboard his ship. They have been visiting relatives. He hopes the voyage will be safer with a soldier on deck. There is valuable wine and oil to deliver but with a blue sky and a warm breeze, it all feels very peaceful for Agathon – he is happy to be on his way home.

Lykon

Ambrosia

Zoe

Hektor

Ariston

Lykon's ship is called Medusa. She carries wine and olive oil.

Poseidon was the god of the sea and the brother of Zeus, the sky father. He could make stormy or calm weather.

Each city-state had their own navy. Greek warships were not rowed by slaves but by free men.

The powerful Athenian navy rules the waves!

The eye keeps the ship safe from evil.

The pointed prow can ram other ships.

Agathon

Greeks stored and transported oil and wine in large pottery jars called amphorae.

Sunken Ancient Greek merchant ships have been discovered on the seabed still loaded with wine and olive oil.

CAMPFIRE STORIES

They camp for the night on a tiny Greek island. Ariston, a travelling teacher, is going to teach Ambrosia's little brother when they get home. He is a good storyteller and, under a sky heavy with stars, he tells them about the Greek hero Odysseus.

In Homer's story *The Odyssey*, Odysseus got lost on his journey home from the Trojan wars and had many scary adventures with monsters.

Odysseus overcame giants and witches to get home. Then, disguised as a beggar, he killed the enemies who had taken his kingdom.

"A hungry cyclops called Polyphemus shut Odysseus' crew in his cave. Every night when he came home with his sheep he would eat some of the sailors. Odysseus made an escape plan. When the cyclops was asleep he drilled a burning stick into his eye!

Odysseus and his men escaped by hanging under the bellies of the sheep. The blind giant could not feel them as they left the cave."

Odysseus was just one of many Greek heroes. Another was Jason, who stole a golden sheepskin and had to fight an army of skeleton warriors!

The Ancient Greeks believed the gods looked down on their lives, sometimes playing with them like pawns in a game of chess.

The sun is very hot today.

Amphora of wine

Amphora of olive oil

Hundreds of Greek islands meant good business for merchants. But also lots of sailing to and fro with deliveries.

Wine and olive oil could be sold many times – from merchant to dealer to market stall and finally to the customer.

DELIVERIES

At their home port of Aegina, Ambrosia and Hektor watch Agathon unloading the deliveries. He heaves the amphorae on to the quayside while Lykon does the wheeling and dealing. Agathon is enjoying himself – in fact, he wonders if there might be a permanent job going…

Watch your back!

Amphora jars are very heavy!

Aegina has a busy port.

Lykon sells the wine and oil to another merchant.

Merchant ships traded their wares as far and wide as Spain and Ancient Egypt.

Aegina was famous for its silver coins shaped like little turtles – and also for the speed of its athletes.

HOME LIFE

Safely home after the long voyage, Lykon has invited Agathon to his house for a meal – bread, oil, goat's cheese and honeyed figs. Then Lykon is taking Agathon to the theatre – he has a suggestion he hopes the big warrior will like...

drying herbs

Lykon's home

family goat

Zoe's making bread and Hektor is playing with his yo-yo.

wasps like honeyed figs too!

Women and men ate separately in different parts of the house. Food was fairly plain – porridge, bread, olive oil and goat's milk.

Every family owned a goat for milk and cheese – even those who lived in towns.

The men are dining in the **andron** (dining room).

They drink wine from flat bowls called **Kylix**.

They eat reclining on **kliines**.

A slave is serving wine with a ladle.

A slave is playing the **diaulos, a double flute.**

Bzzzzzzzz!

Bread dipped in olive oil

goat's cheese

olives

figs

Honey, fresh figs and other fruit were the sweet snacks of the day.

The Greeks thought it was wrong to eat domestic animals unless they had first been sacrificed to the gods.

Agathon is delighted at Lykon's suggestion!

THEATRE

Under the blue sky, actors are performing the tragic tale of Helen of Troy. As Agathon enjoys the drama, Lykon suggests that Agathon might like to join his family business – by marrying Ambrosia!

This play is all about Helen of Troy. It is a tragedy about jealousy and war.

the wooden horse of Troy

Stepped seating means that everyone can see and hear clearly.

The Iliad tells us that Helen, a Spartan queen, ran off with a prince of Troy. Her angry husband attacked the city of Troy with a large Greek army.

The cunning Greeks built a huge wooden horse and left it at the gates. Warriors were hiding inside and once they were in the city, they killed everyone.

All roles are played by male actors - even the females!

a comedy mask

a tragic mask

a fool

a villain

Comedians have big bright padded costumes and platform shoes so they can be seen from far away.

Girls were usually married by the age of 12. The bride's father arranged the wedding with the groom's father, or with the groom if his father had died.

The bride's father would negotiate a 'dowry' with the groom's father, an amount of money offered to 'buy' the bride a husband.

TEMPLE OF THE GODS

Meanwhile Ambrosia walks to the temple. Craning her neck to look up at the breathtaking statue of the goddess Athena, she gives thanks for her safe journey and makes a shy, secret prayer. She won't tell anyone what she asked for – not even us!

Look at the huge gold and ivory statue of Athena, goddess of war and wisdom.

Huge columns hold up the temple.

It's hot and bright outside but in here it's lovely and cool!

The most famous temple in Athens was called the Parthenon. Its ruins survive today. It was built a generation after the time of our story.

The Ancient Greeks believed their gods lived on Mount Olympus and were led by Zeus, who could throw thunderbolts.

Athena

Nike, goddess of victory

Ambrosia

Athena, daughter of Zeus, was the powerful goddess of war and wisdom. She helped humans – or sometimes hurt them if she felt insulted.

Other gods included Apollo, the sun god; Hades, god of the underworld; Hera, goddess of marriage; and Aphrodite, goddess of love.

SCHOOL DAYS

Ariston has so much to teach Hektor: the Greek alphabet, mathematics, handwriting and philosophy. But Hektor loves it most when Ariston tells him stories about Greek heroes. Today he is telling him the very scary story of Theseus and the Minotaur.

Α Alfa
Β Beta
Γ G/N Gamma
Δ D Delta
Ε E Epsilon
Ζ Z/D2 Zeta
Η E Eta
Θ Th Theta
Ι I Iota
Κ K Kappa
Λ L Lambda
Μ M Mu
Ν N Nu
Ξ Xi
Ο O Omicron
Π P Pi
Ρ R Rho
Σ S Sigma
Τ Tau
Υ Y Upsilon
Φ Ph Phi
Χ ch Chi
Ψ PS Psi
Ω ō Omega

family altar

Only boys were given an education. They learned philosophy, history and mathematics.

Most Greek girls were only taught sewing, spinning and house management. Although there were some girls who could read...

"The Minotaur was a flesh-eating monster, half bull, half man that lived in a huge maze of tunnels. Every year children were sacrificed. But then, along came a hero, THESEUS, son of the god Poseidon. He went into the maze and after a terrible struggle slaughtered the Minotaur!"

scroll of papyrus

EKTOP

wax slate

wooden toy horse

Spartan girls were all educated. The state thought educated, healthy girls made healthy babies and the best mothers.

Spartan girls could also own property and inherit wealth when women in other Greek states couldn't.

WEDDING DAY

Today is Ambrosia's wedding day! She is sure Athena must have told Aphrodite about her prayer. There has been a great feast at her father's house. Now it's time for the procession to their new home.

Torches to lead the way.

wedding gifts

Wedding celebrations lasted three days with lots of ceremonies such as the young bride giving her old toys to the gods.

The wedding day began with a bath for the bride. After the feast she was given away by her father to her husband.

The wedding guests have just sung: ♫
"All alone a sweet apple reddens on the topmost branch... the apple pickers didn't notice it... they could not reach it!" ♫♫

Hektor holds nuts and figs to shower the couple with.

They all wear crowns of laurel leaves.

The couple travelled by cart to their new home accompanied by family, well-wishers and song.

Few Ancient Greek wedding songs remain, so the one above – written by Sappho, a famous woman poet – is very important to historians.

Sofia plays the lyre - this one is made from a tortoise shell.

GREEK WOMEN

Ancient Greek women have to spend a lot of time at home. Ambrosia has invited some of her friends around to see her new house and exchange gossip. Her mother-in-law, Demetra, lives there too. She is feeding a friend's baby boy – his potty doubles as a high chair!

This chest is full of bundles of spun wool.

cosmetic pot

perfume pot

Ambrosia and Penelope play knuckle bones.

Married women had their own rooms in the house to live, work and have guests round for dinner.

Young girls looked to older married women for advice about everything from spinning to baby care!

Ambrosia's rooms are on the top floor of the house.

Sofia wears a head scarf.

Demetra

baby feeder

Penelope's son

Helen and Ambrosia gossip as they spin the wool.

Ambrosia has a bronze mirror.

knee protector (when preparing wool for spinning)

wool

Highchair and potty at the same time!

Penelope has a new hairstyle today.

Young couples often had a parent or grandparent living with them.

Ancient Greek ceramic potty chairs have actually been discovered.

MARKET PLACE

At the market Agathon is looking at beautiful vases. A philosopher is talking about the legendary Achilles whose famous motto was 'always be the best'. Suddenly Agathon has a crazy idea – he is going to enter the Olympic Games!

Ancient Greece is still famous to this day for its classical sculptures and decoration on vases and bowls.

Ceramics is the word we use to describe pottery. It comes from the Greek word *Keramos*, meaning 'clay'.

Pelagon gives his daily lecture in the shade of the olive tree. Many people gather to listen.

"Achilles' motto was always be the best!"

The potter's workshop... pots in many shapes and sizes.

The pots are dried in the sun then painted before firing in the kiln.

A young apprentice turns the wheel.

Zenon the potter

Adelpha paints beautiful decorations on the pottery.

Greek Philosophers including Plato, Socrates and Pythagoras were the scientists and mathematicians of their day.

In the Trojan wars, Achilles was killed by an arrow shot through his heel. We now call this part of the foot the Achilles tendon.

Sparta became the toughest of the Greek states and won many battles with its 'death or glory' attitude.

All Spartan men had to be soldiers from the age of 8! They lived in camps, not at home with their wives.

SPARTA

Agathon visits the land of the Spartans on his way to the Games. It's a tough place to live. Even little boys have to be soldiers in Sparta. Agathon, who has trained for months for the Games, is shocked to see Spartan girls exercising too. That's not allowed anywhere else in Greece!

these girls enjoy practising their wrestling!

"Go out and steal!"

Spartans knew that healthy girls were healthy mothers. But any weak babies were left out on the hillsides to die.

Spartan boys were encouraged to steal and cheat. Spartan men thought that made them good soldiers.

OLYMPIA

This is Olympia, home of the Olympic Games! Agathon has made a sacrifice to Nike, goddess of victory, asking her to add wings to his heels for the race tomorrow. Now he can relax and watch today's event – the thrilling chariot races.

Agathon has sworn before Zeus and the ten organisers of the festival that he has trained properly.

Javelin

The whips go "crack"

Discus

The hippodrome horse race is 600m long with turning posts at each end.

The Olympics were held in honour of Zeus, father of the gods who lived far away on Mount Olympus.

The Games were held every four years and were supervised by ten organisers who were trained in the rules and regulations of the Games.

32

This is a four horse chariot race – very dangerous!

A truce between all the Greek states meant athletes and spectators could travel safely to Olympia. It was called the Ekecheiria.

But the Games were for male Greek citizens only! Women weren't even allowed to watch – although special women-only games were held sometimes.

THE GAMES

Lykon cheers as the trumpet blares! Agathon sprints for the finishing-line. It's a hard race. Champion sprinters from all over the Greek world are here today. But the speed of the Aeginetans is legendary…

Boxing matches are fought until one man surrenders

…or even dies!

All competitors in the Olympics are naked

It's the third day; time for the running races.

100 oxen were killed as a sacrifice to the gods. The meat was handed out to the crowd.

There were fewer events than in the modern Olympics. Other events included the javelin, discus and boxing.

The sprinting race was the most glorious Olympic event. It was 192 metres (630 feet) long – the length of the *Stadion*.

Olympic champions could expect to be given expensive gifts and become famous in their home state.

Everyone wants to buy wine and olives from an Olympic champion!

END OF THE GREEKS

Ancient Greece lost its independence when it was conquered by King Philip of Macedon and his son Alexander the Great. Alexander spread Greek culture to vast new territories in the East, including countries like Syria and Egypt. In the Hellenistic era (the period after the death of Alexander in 323 BC), his successors divided the Greek world into several large kingdoms. In the next few centuries, the Romans gradually took over these territories. They conquered the last Hellenistic kingdom in 31 BC.

WHAT THE GREEKS LEFT BEHIND...

Much of our alphabet (named after the first two Greek letters *alpha* and *beta*) is based on the Greek alphabet. The Greek myths are still told to this day and are even made into films. Greek philosophy and mathematics are still used and Greek theatre gave us the first dramatic plays. Greek statues and pottery can be found in most museums and if you visit Mediterranean countries like Greece or Turkey you will find amazing ruins to explore for yourself.

GLOSSARY AND INDEX

Andron (page 17) A special room in a Greek house where only men were allowed.

Aphrodite (pages 21 and 24) The goddess of love.

Apollo (page 21) The sun god.

Athena (pages 20, 21 and 24) The goddess of wisdom and war.

Athens (pages 6, 8, 11 and 20) The capital of the Athenian states, in ruins at the time of our story, but later rebuilt.

Athlete (pages 15 and 33) A sportsman or woman.

Bronze (page 8) A soft metal used for tools and weapons before iron was discovered.

Chariot (pages 32 and 33) A wheeled carriage pulled by horses.

Citizen (page 33) Someone who has the right to live in a country.

Discus (page 32) A flat heavy disc thrown by athletes.

Dowry (page 19) Money paid by a bride's father to her husband.

Greek alphabet (pages 22 and 36) The oldest alphabet in use today. Many Greek letters appear in our own modern alphabet.

Greek gods (pages 10, 17, 20, 21, 23, 24 and 32) The Greeks had many gods. Others not mentioned in this story include Pan, a nature god. He was half man, half goat and played the 'pan pipes'. Artemis was the goddess of child birth and of wild places. She hunted with silver arrows.

Greek heroes (pages 12, 13, 22 and 23) The Greeks had many
heroes like Odysseus and Theseus. Perseus was a hero that
killed the snake-haired female monster, Medusa.
Bellerophon tamed the winged horse, Pegasus, and rode it
to kill the fire-breathing monster, the Chimaera.

Hades (page 21) The god of the underworld and the
name of the Greek underworld.

Hera (page 21) The goddess of marriage.

Herodotus (page 9) A Greek writer and philosopher.

Hippodrome (page 32) An open-air stadium.

Homer (page 12) A famous Greek poet who wrote *The Iliad*
and *The Odyssey*.

Hoplite (page 7) A Greek soldier.

Javelin (page 32) A type of spear.

Kiln (page 29) A sort of oven where pottery is fired.

Knuckle bones (page 26) A game like modern 'jacks'.

Leg guards (page 8) Shin pads to protect the legs
in battle.

Marathon (pages 6 and 9) A famous land battle.

Mount Olympus (page 20) The home of the gods.

Nike (pages 21, 32 and 35) The goddess of victory
and also the Greek word for 'victory'.

Olive oil (pages 10, 11, 14, 16 and 17) A luxury food oil
made from olives.

Olympic Games (pages 28, 31, 32, 33, 34, 35 and 36)
Games originally held in honour of the god, Zeus,
at Olympia.

Papyrus (page 23) The first paper made from reeds.

Parthenon (page 20) A famous Greek temple complex
built after our story when Athens was rebuilt.

Persia (pages 6, 8 and 9) A country which is
today's Iran.

Philosophy (pages 6, 22, 28, 29 and 36) The study
of knowledge and truth.

Plataea (pages 6 and 9) A famous land battle.

Plato (page 29) A famous philosopher.

Politics (page 6) The study of government.

Poseidon (pages 10 and 23) The god of the sea.

Pythagoras (page 29) A mathematician and philosopher.

Quay (page 15) A harbour.

Salamis (pages 6, 8 and 9) A famous sea battle.

Sappho (page 25) A female writer considered to be
one of the greatest of the early Greek poets.

Socrates (page 29) A famous philosopher.

Sparta (pages 8, 18, 23, 30 and 31) A Greek state.

Trireme (page 10) A Greek warship with three sets
of oars.

Troy (pages 12, 18 and 29) A Greek colony (in today's
Turkey). The citizens of this colony were called
Trojans.

Truce (page 32) An agreed peace.

Wax Slate (page 23) A writing tablet.

Zeus (pages 10, 20, 21 and 32) Ruler of the Greek gods.